CONTENTS

First published in 1979

'JUST ONE MORE' STORIES

ILLUSTRATIONS BY

ERIC KINCAID

BRIMAX BOOKS

CAMBRIDGE ENGLAND

PERVIE THE PIGLET

Priscilla was a fine pig. Whenever Farmer Biggs entered her and her piglets in a show she was awarded the first prize. She always had ten piglets in a litter and they were always pink and perfect.

Her last family, though, was of eleven and that extra one really was the odd one out. Instead of doing what his brothers and sisters did he went his own way and found his own amusements. His most noticeable trick was running round and round the pigsty. The farmer's little daughter, Kate, called him 'Pervie' because he was so perverse – always doing the opposite to what he should be doing. Even Priscilla used the name.

"Pervie," she grunted. "Could you possibly put yourself in a more pleasing position?"

She always talked like that – very fond of using words beginning with 'p' for 'pig'.

"Pervie, Pervie. . . .You are the most perplexing piglet. . . . My poor head is pounding with your prancing performances!"

Pervie didn't understand half she said but he loved to hear all her strange expressions. In fact, he thought up more tricks to see if she knew more words.

Kate had named him well – very well indeed.

One day, he made a discovery; he noticed that their sty was not the only world. Outside the bars of the iron gate there stretched another; a much wider one. Out there animals and birds were free; they roamed about doing exactly as they pleased.

That was the life for him. . . .But how could he get to that fine free world?

He pushed his little snout through the railings and wriggled. It wasn't going to be easy. Almost immediately, a sharp pain struck at the middle of his curly tail. He edged himself back into the sty. Priscilla was holding on tight and she didn't let go until he was safely down on all four trotters.

She fixed him with a disapproving eye.

"Pervie," she began in a stern voice. "Put that particular pastime right out of your mind. We are prize pigs. We are preserved and perfected here in this clean sty. This is our special place and you must be satisfied."

But Pervie wasn't satisfied.

Next time he squeezed his rear end through first; this way he could keep watch on his mother. It was a clever idea, but it didn't work.

Priscilla spotted what he was up to and pulled him back by his ear.

Kate heard Pervie squeal and saw his mother holding on. She called to her father.

"I think Priscilla has turned against Pervie, Dad. She was biting him!"

Farmer Biggs examined the piglet.

"You're right, Kate. She's split his ear!"

Poor Pervie. . . .He was no longer perfect. . . .He couldn't be entered for the show.

"May I have him, Dad?" Kate asked.

So, Pervie left the sty and joined the outside world. He was Kate's pet and although he missed his mother at first, he soon put Kate in her place and followed her everywhere.

A few days before the Agricultural Show, a new item was added as an attraction for the children. 'Odd and unusual pets' it said. 'Bring them along and win a prize!'

"I'll take Pervie," said Kate.

So Pervie went to the show after all.

He had to endure a good clean up and being enclosed in a makeshift sty. This didn't please him at all. The judging was about to begin when Pervie decided he'd had enough. Rooting under the insecure hurdles, he dislodged them and was off!

"What perfect, peautiful pleasure!" he whispered to himself, trying to talk like Priscilla. Some faint scent in the air reminded him of her. He was reminded also of his old tricks and he started to race round and round and round!

In no time at all there was chaos!

Children screamed; old people were knocked off balance and show officials ran about shouting and looking ridiculous.

Pervie was the star turn of the afternoon.

When the crowds saw how funny it was they let out a roar of laughter. This grew and spread across the field as Pervie widened his racing circles.

Suddenly, he altered course; turned completely and made a bee-line in the opposite direction. It was even more hilarious – chasers scattered as the pink object dived between their legs.

Far out, across the show ground, he came up sharp against some strong, well-staked fencing. A ticket 'First Prize' hung on a spoke. There lay Priscilla and ten perfect piglets.

Oh, how delighted he was to see her. His ears flapped and trembled with joy – even the torn one. He pushed and pushed his nose into her pen and she met him with tender little grunting noises. While she kissed him on his tender little snout, Pervie stood quite still – but his tail went round faster and faster.

Kate was the first to catch up with him; she grabbed him firmly and popped him in with his mother.

The people cheered. Then, many asked how it was that a pig with a family would accept another – a strange piglet. Kate had to tell the story over and over: that Pervie *was* her piglet and that he had been clever enough to find her.

When it came to the choosing of the most unusual pet; well, Pervie's name was shouted by all the onlookers.

"Pervie! Pervie. . . .He's the one. . . .Pervie!"

The crowd joined in the chant. The judge agreed.

"For entertaining us so well," he said, "I present Pervie with the prize. Piglet of the famous, well-known Priscilla, he has this afternoon, proved himself to be the most pleasing and most peculiar pet of the show."

·Pervie was listening. 'Hallo,' he thought, 'my mother is not the only one who talks like that. . . .And who's peculiar anyway?'

He straightened his tail, curled it up again and gave a little grunt – his very first!

He'd added to his mother's reputation. Her perverse piglet had won a prize! Things were pretty good.

"Yes," he said. "Everything is positively perfect!"

NO BUTTER FOR HIS BREAD

It was breakfast time and the Master wanted butter for his bread.

"Molly!" he called to the dairy maid, "Bring me butter for my bread."

"I can't sir," said Molly.

"Can't!" said the Master. "No such word as can't," and then he added, "Why can't you?"

"Because there is no butter," said Molly.

"No butter!" The Master jumped from his chair and knocked it with a clatter to the floor. "No butter. . . .what do you mean NO BUTTER!!!!"

"There is no butter in the dairy. There is no butter in the kitchen," said Molly.

She righted the Master's chair. He sat down again and glared. He didn't frighten Molly. She knew he was gentle as butter himself underneath his crusty outside. And she knew how much he liked butter on his bread.

"Why isn't there any butter?" he stormed.

"Because. . . ." said Molly. "Because. . . ."

"You're the milk maid. . . ." roared the Master, "Go to the dairy and make me some." He was getting hungry and he couldn't eat bread without butter. He knew he was getting bad tempered. He didn't like being bad tempered.

"Sir," said Molly as though he wasn't shouting at all. "I've been in the dairy since six. The cream in the churn will not turn into butter."

"Don't be ridiculous!" shouted the Master. And jumping from his chair, again knocking it to the floor with a clatter, he marched to the dairy with his napkin caught on his waistcoat button, and with Molly running after him not in the least flustered.

The dairy was cool and airy, and it cooled the Master's temper. "I'm sorry I shouted Molly," he said, "But you know how I like my butter. . .and you really mustn't say there isn't any butter when all you have to do is churn it. Now be a good girl and start churning. . ."

"Very well," said Molly. If the Master wouldn't believe her then he would have to see for himself.

"Surely it's ready now," said the Master who was pacing backwards and forwards in front of Daisy the cow so quickly that she was beginning to wonder if she should toss him over the moon. "Here. . .let me look." Molly took the lid off the churn. The cream from Daisy's milk was pale as the palest primrose and as fluid as the water in the pond.

"What's the matter with it?" demanded the Master.

"What's the matter with your milk?" he demanded of Daisy the cow.

Daisy looked at him with her large brown eyes and mooed. Her moo could have meant anything.

"What's to be done?" demanded the Master.

"Well it seems to me as though it has had a spell put on it," said Molly.

"Spell. . .rubbish!" said the Master.

"Then why won't it turn?" asked Molly.

"Well, what are you waiting for? How do you break a spell?" asked the Master impatiently. He was getting so hungry for bread and butter he was prepared to believe anything and try anything.

"We could try holding it over running water?" said Molly.

That's how it was that the Master's wife found the Master standing in the middle of the stream in the middle of the meadow holding a milk churn over his head.

"Come out of there at once, your feet are getting wet," she scolded.

The Master did as he was told and water and fishes poured from his shoes.

"Drat," he said, as he shook the churn. "It's still sloshing about."

He thought he had better explain to his wife who was dropping the stranded fish back into the stream.

"There's a spell on the milk. It won't churn. I haven't had breakfast. I'm hungry. I want my bread and butter. What shall I do?"

"Tie a rowan sprig to it, dear," said his wife sweetly. "Everyone knows that's how a spell is broken."

There just happened to be a rowan tree close by the dairy. But a sprig tied to the churn made not the slightest difference to the milk.

"So that always works, does it?" said the Master huffily. "What else always works?"

"Horseshoes over the dairy door," said the Master's wife.

There were so many horseshoes over the dairy door there wasn't room for another one.

The Master's wife wanted her husband to buy her a new dress, so she just had to think of something. She thought and thought and could think of nothing. Molly sat beside her and thought and thought and also thought of nothing. The Master churned and churned till his arms ached and his hair was wet with perspiration.

"Who would want to put a spell on a churn of milk?" he panted as he stopped to catch his breath. "It's no one who likes butter that's for sure!"

Molly and the Master's wife looked at one another. Both knew exactly what the other was thinking.

"Molly," said the Master's wife. "Get your bonnet."

"Where are you going?" asked the Master.

"To visit the witch who lives at the mill," said his wife.

"Don't be silly. She likes butter. I've heard she likes butter as much as I do."

"Liking has nothing to do with it," said his wife. "Having, has. . .and I've heard that her butter churn fell over and broke into a hundred pieces."

"Stuff and nonsense," muttered the Master, and went back to his own churning.

Molly and the Master's wife went straight to the mill before their courage failed them. Neither of them would have dared to go alone.

"Yes," said the witch when they questioned her, very politely and very carefully, of course. It doesn't do to upset a witch. "My butter churn IS broken and I can't find the right spell to mend it. I have put a spell on all the unbroken churns. I have no butter so no one else shall."

"Yes," said the witch. "I will take off the spell if you promise to bring me a large pat of freshly made butter every other day."

When Molly and the Master's wife got home, the Master was dancing a jig in the dairy and Daisy was mooing.

"I did it. . .I found the answer. . .it's turned to butter."

"No, you didn't," said the Master's wife. "Now you go straight this minute and take some of that butter to the witch at the mill."

"Why? Why should I?" demanded the Master. But of course, as soon as his wife told him why he should he scooped some into a bowl. He ran all the way to the mill and left it on the witch's doorstep and then he ran all the way home again and had a late breakfast, while his wife went to town and bought a new dress and Molly swept out the dairy and crooned to Daisy the cow.

PEAS

A gardener kneeling on his knees
Planted several rows of peas.
The sunshine shone, the breezes blew,
And all the little peapods grew.

Then, in the night, from a nearby hole,
A family of mice to the garden stole.
They climbed the stems with the greatest ease,
And that was the end of the garden of peas!

BIG BALL

The big ball bounced from off the floor,
The big ball bounced straight out of the door;
The big ball bounced through the garden gate,
The big ball bounced along the street.
Farther and farther, up and down,
The big ball bounced right through the town;
It bounced along the country lanes,
It bounced through several window panes.
Along the river, up the hill,
Through the meadow, by the mill;
Higher and higher it bounced, and soon
It landed on the rising moon.

JUST IN TIME

Squire George was a part-time wizard. Sometimes he was mostly squire and went about his business in the village. Sometimes he was mostly wizard and practised spells from his spell book and did a little bit of magic here and there. And sometimes he was neither squire, nor wizard, but was himself and rode out on his horse just to feel the sun on his face and the wind blowing through his hair.

One day, he had been sitting at his magic spell book for so long his head began to ache.

"I think I'll go for a gallop on my horse," he said and he pushed the spell book to one side.

It didn't take long to put on his riding boots and saddle up his horse.

"Take it steady," he said to his horse as they trotted up the steep hill behind the village. Once at the top it was a different story. The hill stretched for miles with bouncy grass underfoot and clouds racing overhead.

"Gee up there," cried the Squire. With a glad whinny the horse kicked up his heels and they were off.

Down in the village little Billy was bent on mischief. He could see the tiny silhouette of the Squire and his galloping horse up on the hill.

"He'll be up there for hours," he said. "Now is my chance to steal his book of spells." And first making sure that there was no one to observe him he crept along the lane and up the path towards the Squire's big house. He pushed open the door and crept inside. It was still, and very quiet, with not even a ticking clock to break the silence.

He pushed open the study door. There was a book with its pages lying open on the desk. Was that it?

He paused, and waited and listened. He didn't want to be caught in the act of taking it.

Up on the hill, something made the Squire feel prickly behind his ears and down the back of his spine. There was something wrong. . .somewhere.

"Whoa!" he cried to his horse. They pulled up sharply at a point where they could see the rooftops of the village and the roof of the Squire's own house.

He remembered he had left his book of spells open on his desk. Suppose. . .just suppose someone got hold of it. Someone who didn't understand how careful you had to be with magic spells. The damage might be so awful it could never be repaired. He couldn't remember locking the front door either. Perhaps there was someone stealing his book at this very moment.

He had to get home quickly. He whispered to his
horse and they took the quickest way down, which happened
to be straight over the rooftops. They nearly fell
and broke all their bones when the horse's hoof caught
one of the pinnacles on the church tower, but by a firm
strong pull on the reins on the part of the Squire and
a frantic kick by the horse they managed to land
bumpily, but safely.

The Squire ran to his house. He was only just in time. Little Billy was just sneaking out of the front door with the spell book under his arm.

"Mine, I believe," said the Squire. And Billy found himself without the spell book and sitting in the fish pond with a waterlily tucked over his ear and a toad croaking at his elbow. . .

"Oh..oh.." he moaned. "He'll turn *me* into a toad. . . I know he will. . ." The Squire didn't say he would and he didn't say he wouldn't. Instead he looked at Billy sternly and said, "Go home, boy." Which Billy did, trailing water weed and waterlilies from his breeches.

As for the Squire, he was so relieved to have saved the village from disaster, that he resolved from that day onwards always to keep his book of spells under lock and key, and that is just what he did.

A PIECE OF ROPE

I've slung a rope up in a tree,
It's hanging from a branch;
But when I mount and swing away
It's my stallion on the ranch.

He's swift and strong, a champion;
My friend, so sure and true;
We'll track down all the 'baddies'
Like cowboys in Westerns do.

We help to drive the cattle,
We cross the scorching plain;
We outshoot any ambush
Set up to kill for gain.

Then when we've made our journey,
And arrive 'all-in' – work done,
I tether up my splendid steed
And put away my gun.

If the 'baddies' ever get me
I'll be very brave – I hope;
But of course it's only a lovely game;
And my horse – just a piece of rope!

NED OF THE TODDIN

Once upon a time, there was a little tortoiseshell kitten with pointed ears and a twitchy tail. His name was Ned of the Toddin, which was rather a strange name, but it was the only one he had, and he soon got used to it. His mother's name was Waowhler, and his father's name was Skaratch, and they all lived together on an emerald green bank between an old stone farmhouse and a brambly wood.

Now you could tell that Ned of the Toddin was not an ordinary kitten, because he began to look out for mice when he was only two hours old. When he was only two days old, he could skip about and talk better than most grown-up cats. When he was only three days old he was a full-size furry kitten, and when he was four days old he began to go out on his adventures.

First of all he trotted daintily up to the old stone farmhouse when nobody was about, just to see what it was like. There on the grey stone step were three bottles of snow-white milk with shiny silver tops.

"Give me some milk," cried Ned, "or I'll knock your tops off with my twitchy tail."

But the milk bottles just stood there, as deaf as three white posts, and didn't do anything at all. So Ned went up to the first milk bottle and carefully pressed its silver top with his twitchy tail. Then he took it between his furry paws and drank all the milk out of it. GULP. GULP. GULP. Just like that. Then he went up to the second milk bottle and pressed its silver top carefully with his twitchy tail. Then he took it between his furry paws and drank all the milk out of that too. But when he came to the third, he had really had enough, so he drank no more than the smooth cream off the top. LAP. LAP. LAP. Just like that. It was delicious. When the farmer came to look for his milk he was very surprised indeed to find most of it gone.

"Well I don't know," he said.

In the meantime, Ned of the Toddin went skipping gaily over the emerald green grass towards the sparkling river that ran along behind the farmhouse. Now an ordinary kitten is very frightened indeed of water, but Ned didn't mind it a bit. There he stood, on the riverside, and as he looked down into the sparkling water he could see a lot of little fish swimming lazily about in the sunshine, for all the world as if it was a Sunday, with nothing to do.

"Come up and be eaten, little fish," cried Ned, "or I'll splash all of the water out of the river with my twitchy tail."

But the little fish were far too busy doing nothing to listen to Ned, and they just went on swimming lazily about in the sunshine.

"Come up and be eaten, little fish," cried Ned again, "or I'll knock all your scales off with my twitchy tail."

But the little fish could not hear what Ned was saying. They just went on swimming round and round in the sparkling water. So Ned jumped straight into the river and gobbled up all the lazy fish. GOBBLE. GOBBLE. GOBBLE. Just like that.

Then he sprang merrily out of the water onto the river side. He shook himself so hard that the little water drops made a rainbow in the sunshine.

"That's better," he said.

Then he went on his way for all the world like an ordinary kitten who is simply out for a stroll among the daisies and dandelions.

He hadn't gone very far when he came upon a rather muddy pigsty. Inside the pigsty was a very large pig indeed. He had pink flapping ears, and pink trotters, and a curly pink tail. His name was Groanergut Swilltrough, and he was the most bad-tempered pig in the neighbourhood. As soon as he saw Ned he gave an unfriendly little grunt. GHHHH. Just like that.

"Go away, little kitten," he said. "I haven't got time for you today." Groanergut kicked several pieces of mud at Ned as he stood in the entrance to the pigsty.

"If you do that again," said Ned. "I'll knock your ears flat with my twitchy tail."

Groanergut Swilltrough gave a horrid little squeal. EEEEE. Just like that. Then he kicked some much larger pieces of mud at Ned. Any ordinary kitten would have run away, but Ned was not an ordinary kitten by a long way. All he did was hit Groanergut's piggy nose with his twitchy tail. WOP. Just like that.

"SQUEEEEEAL!" said Groanergut, looking very shocked indeed.
He got as much mud as he could, and tried to kick it over Ned,
but Ned skipped cleverly out of the way, and it all missed. Then
Groanergut ran up to Ned, and tried to squash him into the mud, but
Ned pulled his flapping ears over his eyes with his twitchy tail, so
that he couldn't see where he was going. He bumped into the side of
the pigsty with a terrible THUD. Just like that.

"EEEEEE," said Groanergut. He lay there exhausted.

In the meantime, Ned of the Toddin went happily on his way across
the emerald green grass, all sprinkled on with snow-white daisies.
He went past the old stone farmhouse, and he was just on his way home
when he smelled a delicious smell. He sniffed, and sniffed again,
but he didn't know what it was because he was only four days old, and
you couldn't expect him to know *everything*. SNIFF. SNIFF. SNIFF.
He followed the smell all the way back to the old farmhouse. It led
him over the grey stone step, and into the spotless white kitchen.

There, on the wooden table, was a beautiful piece of yellow cheese.
Ned sniffed carefully. No doubt about it. The smell led right up
to the cheese. Quick as a flash Ned jumped onto the table and ate up
the cheese. SWILLOWSWALLOW. Just like that.

"That was delicious," he said.

Just then he heard someone coming, so he jumped straight down off the wooden table and went quietly out through the door. When the farmer's wife saw that her cheese had gone she was very surprised indeed.

"Well I don't know," she said.

As soon as he got home, Ned the Toddin told his mummy and daddy all he had done during the day. Skaratch and Waowhler raised their furry eyebrows, because they had never heard of such an extraordinary kitten before.

"Well," said Skaratch.

"Well," said Waowhler.

So Ned curled up on a patch of soft moss and went to sleep, because he really was a bit tired after his adventures. There he lay, in a little tortoiseshell bundle, for all the world like a quiet well-behaved kitten of whom any mother could be proud.

"PRRRRRR," he said. "PRRRRRR."

BESSIE THE ELEPHANT

Bessie the elephant blushed with shame;
She had forgotten her name, her name.
She asked the stork, but he would not tell,
The parrot he merely said "Well well."
She asked the lion, who roared with laughter,
And ten little monkeys came giggling after.
She asked the hippo, who yawned aloud,
The stately peacock was much too proud.
The donkey he merely gave a bray,
The dormouse was shy, and couldn't say.
Bess blew her trumpet: "Oh tell me do."
Then all of them answered: "You are you!"

BILLY AND THE MONSTER

Billy sat on the rocks fishing. It was nearly supper time and he'd caught nothing. Suddenly a voice said:

"Will this one do?"

Billy turned to see a monster's head raised up out of the water and a fish flapping on the rocks.

"I'm Jessica," said the monster.

"OH. . .Thank you!. . .I'm Billy. . .Can I do anything for *you*?" Jessica wanted some different food.

"I'm tired of fish," she said.

Billy raced home. He ate his supper and was back at the rock with his pockets bulging. Jessica waited.

"Come for a ride," she said, humping her back. Away they went, Billy singing at the top of his voice and Jessica beating time with her tail.

It was fun. Billy went up and down riding the monster like a rocking horse.

"I'll take you to my island," said Jessica.

Billy could see it in the distance; it looked a wonderful place. When Jessica slid up on to the beach, she lowered her back for Billy to get off. Then she surrounded him with her coiled body.

"Now Billy," she said, "what have you brought me?"

For the first time Billy noticed how beautiful she was. Her big dark eyes with thick lashes, the coloured markings on her silky skin and her gentle voice; they made her someone quite special.

"Oh, yes. . .I have. . ." he stammered. He felt he should say, 'Your Royal Highness', or 'Your Majesty!' He pulled a packet from his pocket almost ashamed of his simple gift.

"I could only bring bread. I hope you like it."

He broke a piece off and held it for her. She took it carefully, eating slowly, tasting it well.

"More, please," she asked.

Billy fed her until the last crust had gone.

"That's all, Jessica. Were you disappointed?"

She smiled: "Not at all, Billy. It was delicious!. . .What did you call it?"

Billy was delighted to have pleased her.

"Bread," he answered.

"Mmm. . .bread," she repeated. The word was new to her. Then she made him a pillow with her tail.

"There, lie down, Billy. You must be tired."

He was soon fast asleep.

Billy awoke to see eyes peeping at him over the wall of Jessica's body. These eyes belonged to crabs, lobsters, an octopus waving her arms about and a smiling dolphin. He liked the dolphin.

"They found crumbs from your bread," said Jessica. "They're hoping for some more."

Billy wished he did have more; but his pockets were empty.

"They want you to make some," went on Jessica. "In fact, they demand it."

Billy could see they were excited and quarrelsome.

"I can't!" he said. "Mother makes it!"

"Shall I bring your mother here?" Jessica whispered.

Billy shook his head. "No, she wouldn't come! Besides, she couldn't make bread here!"

Jessica was thinking.

"Would your mother make bread for me to bring back?" she asked.

"Well. . .Yes," Billy began, "if she had enough flour."

Jessica smiled. "Then my plan will work. I'll promise them bread and leave to get it. You must wait here. I'll turn back and come close in under the water. When you see my tail, jump on and we'll be away." It sounded a good idea.

"Won't they be angry and swim after us?" asked Billy.

Jessica's eyes twinkled.

"They might – but they're slow – except the dolphin and he's a friend."

She raised herself up, looked at them all and made a speech. Some clapped their claws, pleased; others grumbled. The dolphin came to stand by Billy. Jessica pushed out to sea.

"Keep them happy," advised the dolphin. "You were singing last night – start singing now."

Billy was glad to have something to do.

"I'll try," he said. His voice wouldn't come at first but soon he was braver and louder. The dolphin swayed to the music. Before long all the creatures were clapping, tapping and stamping – a real percussion band!

While they were all enjoying themselves, Jessica's tail appeared, slithering towards Billy, from the waves.

"Keep singing," muttered the dolphin, "and go – Now!"

Billy jumped – but stopped singing!

The creatures looked round.

"We've been tricked!" they cried. "You promised us bread! You promised!"

They scuttled down the beach and dived in after Jessica and Billy. Jessica outswam them all. Billy saw his mother out looking for him. He waved and shouted. How amazed she was to see him riding on the back of a monster!

He ran to her and brought her to the water's edge to meet his friend Jessica. They sat talking and Billy's mother said she would be glad to make lots of bread so that Jessica could keep her promise to the sea creatures.

Just then, who should come to join them but the dolphin. He was smiling, looking very happy. He'd persuaded the disappointed crabs, lobsters and the octopus that if only they'd be patient instead of bad tempered, everyone would be satisfied.

Off went Billy and his mother to get the fire going and to make the bread. They were all to meet again that evening.

What a party they had!

Jessica caught fish which Billy cooked on the beach. When his mother brought the crisp, crusty loaves there was a loud cheer. On the rocks, sat all the creatures, waiting for their share. They clapped and praised the excellent food called 'bread'. After supper they entertained one another. The dolphin gave acrobatic leaps out of the water; Billy sang and his mother told them a story.

Jessica had never enjoyed herself so much.

"Please, Billy's mother, may we come again?" she asked.

Everyone laughed and waved. "Yes, yes. . .Do please come again!"

The dolphin whispered, "She's our queen, you know."

Billy's heart bounced! "I knew it!" he muttered. . ."I just knew it!"

SPROGGET

Whenever I feel lonely and the day is dull or sad,
I whisper to my special friend – the best I ever had.
He comes at once – from nowhere; he's ready for a game;
"Hi, Sprogget!" I call out to him, for Sprogget is his name.

He loves to hide up in a tree – he's dressed in shades of green;
With dainty shoes and fitting cap – the smartest to be seen;
And just to add a final touch to clothes of softest leather
There, above a pointed ear, he wears an orange feather.

No one ever sees him: I'm the only one who can;
Because my friend called Sprogget is a magic sort of man.
There's nothing, really, he can't do – at any time of day;
At night he'd fly me to the moon; I've only got to say.

At meal times he's most useful; he helps me eat things up
And when there's milk I have to drink – he shares it from my cup.
I phone him and he rings me back; I know which calls are mine;
But Mummy says, "Wrong number!" when it's Sprogget on the line!

His feelings could be very hurt, when he's cut off like that;
So, then I plan a treat for him – leave presents on the mat.
He never, never lets me down – not on the darkest night;
Perhaps *he's* just a wee bit scared; he always cuddles tight.

We dive beneath the blankets, to our cave below the sea;
Then we pretend we hunt for sharks – fight swordfish – what a spree!
We never seem to come ashore – it's a whole night escapade;
With morning light I'm safe in bed and Sprogget's not afraid.

On shopping days, inside big stores, we have a lot of fun;
My Sprogget he gets up to tricks – and then we have to run.
He muddles people's parcels, at the counter where they pay;
"That's mine!". ."Oh, no!". ."I'm sure!". ."Oh, yes!". . .they all begin to say.

But mostly he is very good – reminds me when to wash,
To clean my teeth and take great care the full bath doesn't slosh.
I guess you wish you had a friend to carry in your pocket:
Start searching now and do not stop – till you have found a Sprogget.

THE UNEXPECTED RAINBOW

High above the earth in the land of clouds there were two kingdoms, the kingdom of Sol, and the kingdom of Splash. Both of these were ruled by powerful kings.

Now the king of Splash lived in a tall, proud castle on top of a big black rain cloud. While not many miles away, on a big, fluffy sun cloud lived the king of Sol.

You would think that living so close to one another, the two kingdoms would be friendly, but this was not so. In fact they were always quarrelling because the king of Splash always wanted it to rain, and the king of Sol always wanted it to be sunny.

So in order to make things fair, the two kingdoms agreed that one day it would be nice and sunny so that people could go for picnics, and the next, it would rain so as to give the trees and flowers a good drink.

For a time this plan worked very well, until one day things went very wrong.

The king of Splash was getting rather old, and at times he was apt to be very forgetful. His memory was getting so bad, that sometimes he even forgot to eat his breakfast.

On this particular morning, the king woke up even more forgetful than usual. He not only forgot to eat his breakfast, but he also forgot which day it was.

By lunchtime he was very hungry, and that made him very grumpy. He went over to the window and looked down at the earth below.

"M m m yes," he said, "things down there look as though they could do with a good drink. We'll give them a good soaking today."

He picked up a small golden bell from his table and shook it hard. Immediately the door opened and a little blue man popped his head inside the room.

"Summon the chief Rainmaker," called the king. "Yes, your Majesty," said the little man and ran off down the stairs.

Two minutes later, another little man popped his head round the door.

"Yes your Majesty?" he said.

"Come in, come in," boomed the king.

The little man came in and closed the door behind him. The king looked out of the window again, then turned to the little man.

"What a lovely day for a downpour, Plip," he said smiling. "I think we'll have a nice shower today."

The little man scratched his head.

"Beg pardon your Majesty," he said, "but it's not supposed to rain today."

"Not supposed to rain!" shouted the king, "If I say it will rain, then it will rain. Is that clear?"

"But your Majesty. . . . ."

"Don't but me," shouted the king feeling very angry indeed. "Go and do as I say!"

The little man backed slowly out of the room. "Yes, your Majesty, certainly your Majesty."

Poor Plip ran down the stairs as fast as his little legs would carry him. When he reached the bottom, he had to climb another flight of steps, and those led him to the Rain Tower. At the top of the Tower was a tiny room and inside this stood the Rainmaker. One good tug at the great wheel was all that was needed, and soon the rain was pitter-pattering down onto the earth below.

The king looked down from his window, and clapped his hands with glee as he watched the large spots of rain send the people on earth running off to find shelter.

But why had they looked so surprised? Surely by now they knew when to expect rain?

Strangely enough, the people on earth were not the only ones surprised at the rain.

A few miles away the people of Sol were gazing out of their windows in astonishment.

"Surely this could not be so," they cried.

"It is our turn to make it sunny today, why, only yesterday it poured with rain."

The king of Sol stood at his window and watched angrily as the rain poured down onto the earth below.

"Summon the Torch Bearer," he shouted, "and light the biggest candle in the castle. That should put a stop to the downpour!"

The sight of the large candle alight made the king of Splash even angrier, and he shook his fist at the great white cloud.

"How dare they," he cried, "HOW DARE THEY." His shouting echoed around the castle.

Startled, Plip came running into the room.

"Ah!" said the king. "The very person I wish to see. Thunder and lightning, that's what we need – I want the biggest thunderstorm possible. That should put their candle out once and for all."

"But your Majesty, you don't understand. . ."

"Go," boomed the king, "do as I say or I shall have you locked up in the deepest dungeon, with nothing to eat but bread and water."

Poor Plip shook in his shoes, then once again turned on his heels and fled to the Rain Tower.

The lightning flashed, the thunder crashed and the rain poured down in torrents.

While on Sol, more candles were lit and never before had they burned as fiercely as they did that day.

As for the people on earth, well, they could hardly believe their eyes. One moment the thunder roared above them and the rain poured down in torrents. The next, the sun shone bright and hot.

The battle went on for some time, although it wasn't long before the strange sight came to the attention of the cold North Wind. He was busy at that moment blowing the snow to people in faraway lands.

Now the cold North Wind being very clever, and also very powerful, realised at once what had happened; so leaving his work immediately, he flew off towards the two kingdoms.

"I'll teach the pair of them," he said angrily. Taking one mighty breath, he blew out all the candles on Sol, and promptly froze the water in the giant Tap on Splash.

The people of Splash looked up at their Rainmaker in horror. A large drop of water had frozen solid around the bottom of the great Tap, and try as they might they could not make it rain.

On Sol too, the people looked up in dismay at the proud golden candles. All that was left of the brilliant yellow light was now just a puff of black smoke.

The people on earth came out of their houses and looked up at the sky. What had happened to the sun, and where was the rain?

These were very strange goings on indeed.

By now, the king of Splash had been told of his mistake, and was feeling very silly. He knew he would have to go and apologise to the king of Sol and make friends with him again.

So he ordered his carriage to be made ready and set off for the big white cloud.

The king of Sol sat on his throne with his head resting on his hand. What was he to do? Perhaps he had been too hasty. After all, the king of Splash was getting old and he had heard that he was rather forgetful at times.

Suddenly there came a loud knock at the door. . .Rap. . .Rap. . .Rap. . .RAAP!

"Humph, come in," he called.

The door opened and there stood the king of Splash.

The king got up from his throne and held out his hands.

"My dear fellow," he cried.

The king of Splash walked up to him and took his hands.

"I've been an old fool," said the king of Splash.

"And I have been too hasty," said the king of Sol.

Suddenly, without warning, came a loud BANG and all the doors of the palace flew open.

"So, I see you have made friends again." It was the North Wind.

"Yes, we have," said the two kings together.

"I see," said the North Wind. Then he thought for a moment.

"Well, do you both solemnly promise never to quarrel again?"

Both kings nodded their heads.

"Very well, in that case I shall send for my brother the warm South Wind, to undo the work I have done."

The North Wind kept his promise and sent for his brother.

One great puff of his warm breath and immediately the water in the giant Tap unfroze, and once again the golden candles of Sol burned bright and hot.

So everything turned out happily in the end and just to show the people on earth that the two kingdoms had made friends, the people of Sol and Splash joined together and painted a giant rainbow across the sky.

LONG AGO

When Granny was a little girl
She bought things in the street;
Muffins from the Muffin Man
And chestnuts for a treat;
Crispy, hot, delicious;
Burning in her hand;
The smell as nuts were roasting
She remembers – it was grand.

Then, there was the Organ Man;
The children gathered round
Laughing at his monkey,
Dancing to the sound;
Tossing him a penny
As the hurdy-gurdy played;
While pennies kept on tinkling
The Organ Man, he stayed.

But Granny liked the man the best
With windmills on his barrow;
Reds and yellows, bright and gay
Whirring in the breeze.
"Oh Mother, Mother!" she would say,
"A jam jar, quickly please!"
Then out to change it for the toy:
To think a jar could buy such joy!

And while she played and chased about
In other streets she'd hear him shout:
"Windmills for jam jars. . .jam jars. . .
jam jars!"
Fading as he went;
And Granny was so happy
With the jam jar she had spent.

CHEESE AND BEES

"Haste away and lock the doors," shouted Martha McGimble as she ran through the village street, her hair falling from its net and the vegetables falling from her basket so great was her hurry. "Haste you away. . .the tinkers are on the road."

At the mention of tinkers everyone in the sleepy village street woke with a start.

"Quick Mary. . .lock up the chickens," shouted Mary's mother.

"Take the pig into the barn and bolt the door," shouted Daniel's father.

The women ran to take in their washing. The men gathered up their rakes and hammers. The children picked up their balls and called to their dogs.

"The tinkers are coming. . .hurry. . .hurry. . ."

Normally the village folk welcomed tinkers. The kind of tinker, that is, who sold pots and pans and stewed his dinner in an old iron pot over a kindling fire. These tinkers, the tinkers they ran from, were tinkers of a different kind. They were tinkers who stole clothes from washing lines, tinkers who broke fences and put other peoples dinners in their cooking pots and other peoples possessions in their pockets. When they were in the village nothing was safe, unless it was locked up or hidden.

The tinkers thought it a lovely joke to frighten so many people all at the same time and they were always raiding the village. Things got so bad that soon no one dared to hang washing out at all. Potatoes couldn't be dug and left to dry in the sun anymore. Chickens could no longer be allowed to peck freely in the long grass.

"Something has to be done about this," fumed Old John, when one day the tinkers crept into the village unnoticed and stole the very chair he was sitting on. "We must consult the wizard."

"Are you sure that will be safe?" asked one of Old John's friends.

"Not for those rascally tinkers I hope," said Old John.

The wizard had lived in the village for many years. The villagers always took great care not to upset him for they didn't quite know what he could do in the way of spells. But he had always been friendly and he had helped them out of trouble before, so Old John and the village elders went to consult him.

"I know why you have come," said the wizard before they could utter a word. "Turn round and go home. Next time the tinkers come to the village close your windows and lock your doors and leave the rest to me."

The village elders went home, not having said a word, but knowing somehow that the wizard understood their problem and would help.

"I can never understand how he knows things without being told," said Old John's wife. "Makes me feel kind of creepy, that does. . ."

It made Old John feel a bit uneasy too.

But not as uneasy as the tinkers felt a few days later. They descended on the village in a noisy, rowdy band. Windows were closed and doors locked in the twinkling of an eye.

"Ha. .ha. .ha. ." laughed the tinker chief. "Someone was in such a hurry he forgot his cheese."

And indeed, standing right where the tinkers couldn't fail to see it, on a three-legged stool to raise it from the ground, was a round, ripe and beautiful cheese.

There was a lot of whispering going on behind locked doors.

"Whose cheese is that?"

"How did that cheese get there?"

"The cheese is mine," said the wizard hobbling from his house, pretending to be afraid. . .which he wasn't.

"Oh no it isn't. . .not any more," said the tinker chief.

"Just let me take one slice," said the wizard, quickly sinking his knife into it's creamy skin.

"Away from there!" shouted the tinker in a temper.

He roughly pushed the wizard to one side, but not before the wizard had whispered something to the cheese.

From the hole which he had just cut rose a thousand humming, buzzing, angry bees, that buzzed and threatened and stung. . .and stung. . .and stung. . .and stung. . .

"Ow . . . ow . . . ow . . ." screeched the tinkers as they took to their heels and ran, with the bees following close behind. The bees may be chasing the tinkers still because neither the bees, nor the tinkers, were ever seen in the village again.

As for the wizard, he went back to his cottage and bothered nobody, and nobody bothered him until there was another problem to solve. That way everyone was happy. Except those rascally tinkers of course.